To You, The Dreamer, Believer, Courageous Reader

First published
in the English language
in 2012 by

Glitterati
INCORPORATED

New York | London

Glitterati Incorporated
New York / London

New York Office:
225 Central Park West
New York, New York 1002
Tel: 212 362 9119

London Office:
1 Rona Road
London NW3 2HY
Tel/Fax: +44 (0) 207 8339

www.GlitteratiIncorporated.com

media@Glitteratiincorporated.com
for inquiries

Follow us on
Facebook and
Twitter at Glitterati Buzz

Library of
Congress Cataloging-in-
Publication data is
available from the
publisher.

Hardcover ISBN 13:
978-0-9832702-3-2

Printed and bound
in China

10 9 8 7 6 5 4 3 2 1

Creative Direction and Illustrations by Julie Muszynski
Design by Belinda Hellinger

Hand Lettering by Sheryl D. Nelson

To Mom and Dad, for your love, support and
a wonderful, once in a lifetime trip...
Asante sana! Ninakupenda!!

A very special thank you to:
My Fairy Grandmother, Harriet

Meg and Al
Lila and Frank

Becky, Liz, Irene,Tim
Marta, Belinda, Sheryl

For more information on
Henley, see
www.henleywoofntails.com

Credits:

World Map ©Hammond Maps

Thank you to The Martin and Osa
Johnson Safari Museum and Conrad
Froehlich for their support and use of
the zebra pattern for the cover as well
as the photographs of Osa Martin
and The Tribesman.

Theodore Roosevelt, Jay Henry
Mowbray, *Illustrious Career and
Heroic Deeds of Col. Roosevelt*

Lion, Camilla Koffler and L.S.B.
Leakey, *Animals in Africa*, Harper and
Brothers

All other images are from the
author's collection. Every effort
has been made to trace the
copyright owners of the material
reproduced here. Any further
information will be gratefully
received and acknowledged.

One morning the elegant and very accessorized Ms. Lulu Ziminski, fashion maven extraordinaire, and Henley, her regal, royal and simply adorable Japanese Chin, received the most exotic invitation from Ms. Lulu's dear, dear, good friend, Baroness Karen Von Dachshund, and this is what it said:

PAR AVION
AEROGRAMME

RHINOCEROS

TANZANIA

Japanese Chin

120/-

Bibi Lulu Ziminski and
Bwana Henley
1 Pedigree Place Penthouse
New York, New York 10000
USA

Dearest Lulu,

Deny Bird Hound and I cordially invite
you and your divine furry friend,
Henley, to join us on a splendid
African adventure, through the majestic
and golden Serengeti Plains to witness
the greatest of great migrations, a
marvelous mingling of the continent's
finest creatures.

Hope you can make it darling, it is
sure to be fun!

R.S.V.P PLEASE,

The Baroness

Thrilled,
Ms. Lulu immediately rang
The Baroness and quickly declared,

"Of course darling, we'd love to be your guests. However, my Henley has just one request."

"Well, out with it," The Baroness promptly replied.

"Henley would like to meet the king of the jungle, that gregarious fellow... You, know that fabulously fickle beast, that only dines on fancy feast!" Ms. Lulu continued.

"Why you mean that bombastic bore, who prides himself on a good ROAR?" said The Baroness.

"Yes, yes.
That's that. A CAT!"
Ms. Lulu exclaimed.

"Oh my!" Shrieked The Baroness,
"But why?"

"You see darling, Henley's relatives
are the legendary Lion Dogs of
Japan. So, naturally he believes he is
part lion!"

"Ahh...But of course," The
Baroness concluded. "It shall be
arranged, I just happen to know
one with the most beautiful
mane. See you soon dear. Ta ta!"

Suddenly, Ms. Lulu heard a
click and before she could
continue on...
The Baroness had gone.

"Oh, Henley!" Ms. Lulu proclaimed. "We are off to a mystical land. Africa, darling, now isn't that grand!"

Delighted, Henley leaped down and spun around.

Wagging his fluffy white tail, he tossed his head back with all his might, B U T, instead of the luminous lion's call he hoped to do, out came a measly "Woo Woo Woooooooo!"

Ms. Lulu gracefully glided over to her precious pet, patting him lightly on his head, she said,

"Not to worry, my petit le chien lion, one day you too shall find your voice." Then softly she tapped her hand on his heart, "You just have to believe in your self." In the meantime, sweetheart, I have arranged for your dream to come true... You are going to meet a lion or two!"

Henley looked up at Ms. Lulu with his big brown eyes; he raised his ears slightly and cocked his head to the right. Why, he was going to learn to ROAR just like his ancestors did before him!

It was here, on one of their afternoon strolls that Ms. Lulu and Henley's curiosity with Africa first began, when they stumbled upon a remarkable portrait that caught their eyes. Its uncanny resemblance was quite a surprise!

OF NATURAL HISTORY

Before traveling to Africa, there is
so much to do...
And, Oh yes ...

PACK!

Henley's List
Dig Up Bones
Fetch Monkey

My Lulu's list
Unearth Passports
Get Vaccinations
Secure Visas
Ring Travel Agent
Confirm Airline Tickets
Verify Hotel Reservations
Locate Itinerary & Maps
Locate "DOOM" Insect Repellent
Leave copy of Itinerary with
    Mr. Allbite Snifferson Tall
Look for Swahili Phrase Book
Find Proper Safari Attire
Prepare International Luggage Tags

PASSPORT

United States
of America

CANINE
PASSPORT

United States
of America

BASIC SWAHILI

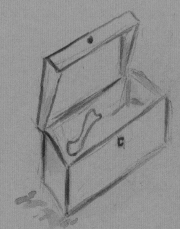

Baroness Von Dachshund kindly arranged for Ms. Lulu and Henley to see her personal friend, the marvelous fashion designer, Monsieur Ruff Roar'n.

Everyone who is anyone knows Ruff makes the most exquisite safari clothes.

"For you, Ms. Lulu, I have designed jodhpurs and a fabulous hat that also doubles as a mosquito net," Ruff yapped. He turned to Henley and said with a woof, "VOILA, mon petit Henley, a coat with boots!"

Au Revoir!

And so Ms. Lulu, dressed in her finest zebra printed coat, and Henley, sporting his 100% purest of pure silk scarf, packed their bags, donned their aviator goggles, waved good-bye to the doorman, and...

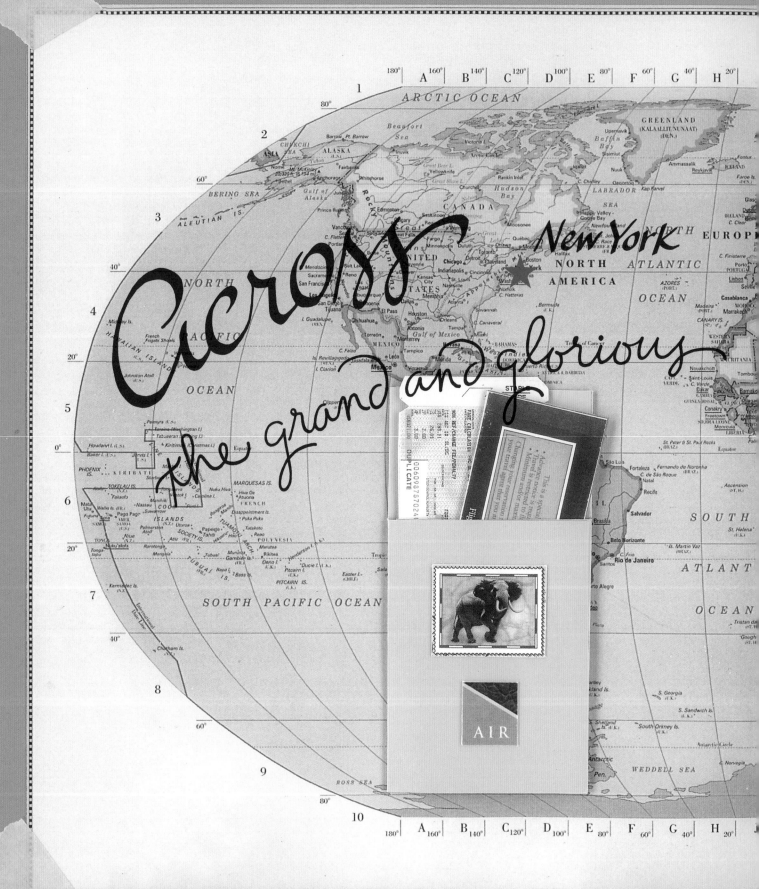

Across New York
the grand and glorious

Atlantic Ocean

Kenya

they flew!

"Jambo Bibi Lulu and Bwana Henley! Welcome to AFRICA!"

Ms. Lulu tossed her arms into the air and waved. Batting her eyes, she brilliantly replied, "Why, Barkley Livingston, I presume. The Baroness has told us so much about you."

"Karibu!" Barkley barked. "Baroness Von Dachshund sent me to fetch her guests. She also mentioned our Bwana Henley had a very special request."

"Yes, darling. You see Henley pawsitively dreams of learning that magical, magnificent and monumental call of the jungle!" Henley wagged his tail and agreed.

Jambo!

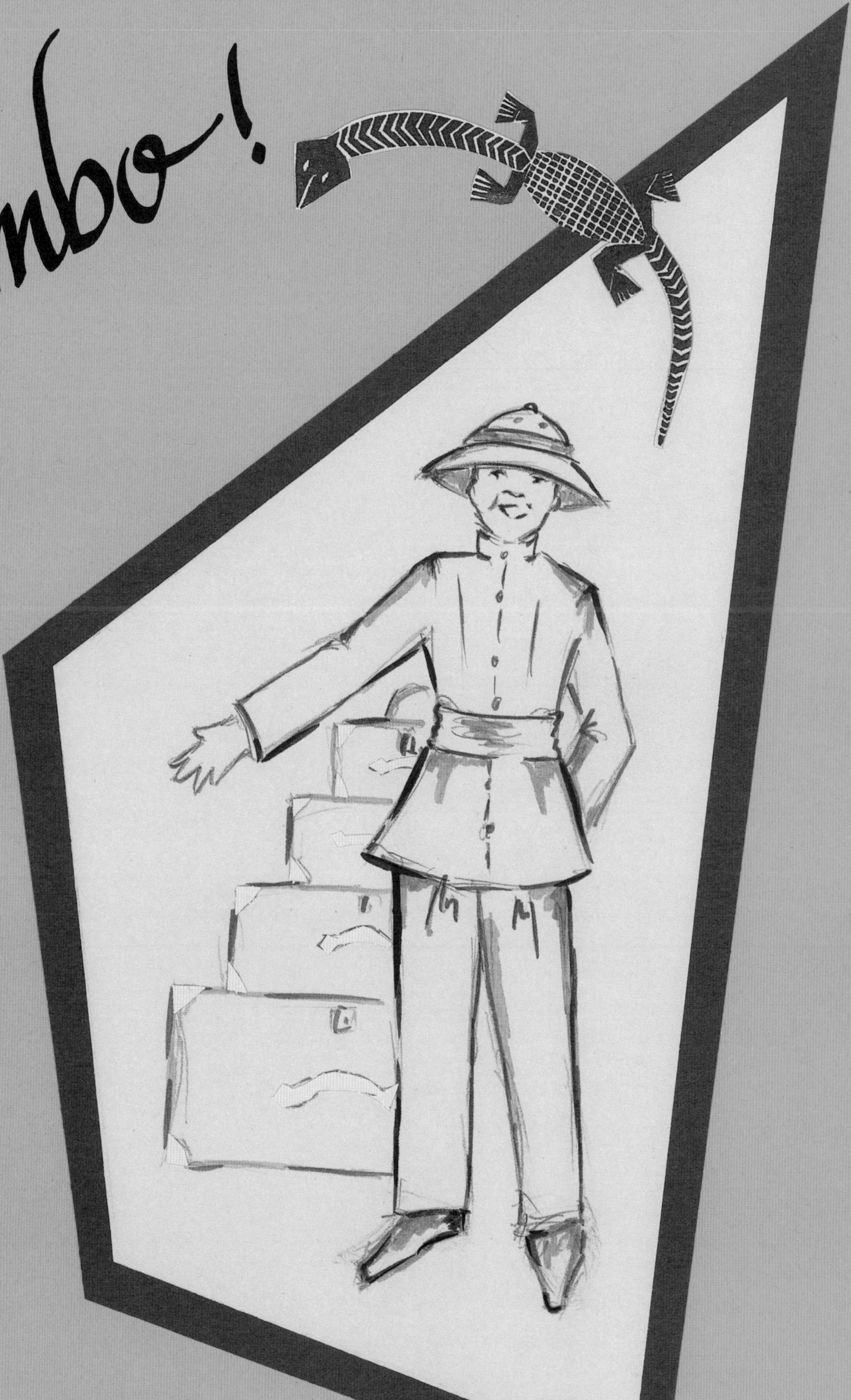

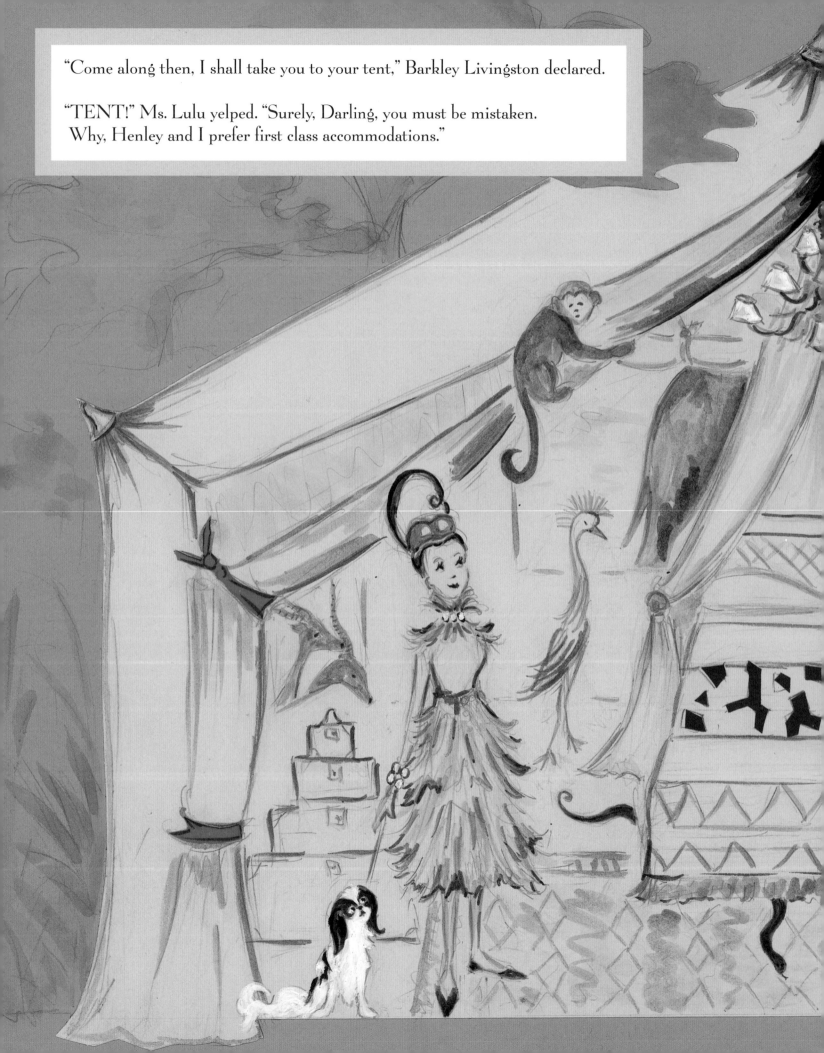

"Come along then, I shall take you to your tent," Barkley Livingston declared.

"TENT!" Ms. Lulu yelped. "Surely, Darling, you must be mistaken. Why, Henley and I prefer first class accommodations."

"Certainly, Ms. Lulu, I do understand." Barkley Livingston assured her, "The Baroness prefers only the finest for her guests, a lavish tent from The Lion's Den. See you two tomorrow, five a.m. Settle in!"

The next morning Ms. Lulu and Henley heard a loud bangity, bang, clang, clang and out of a plume of dust suddenly appeared, a rattling Range Rover, with Barkley Livingston at the wheel.

Abruptly the safari vehicle came to a halt. Out popped none other than the dashing Denny Bird Hound himself, while the Baroness frantically waved her arms from above. Blowing gigantic kisses to her guests she howled, "Muah! Muah! Muah! Helloooooo! Jambooo!"

"Good morning!" Denny said to Ms. Lulu and Henley. "Your exotic safari is about to begin. Please do hop in!" Then he turned to little Henley and with a quick wink he barked, "I understand you would like to meet a Lion my friend? Well, keep your eyes wide open and remember, paws in!"

They drove for miles and miles across the golden Serengeti Plains, now and then seeing the Maasai tribesmen all dressed in red.

Continuing down the dusty path, the nomads came upon quite a surprise, two of the coveted and prized "Big Five".

"The Rhino and Elephant are both utterly enormous... totally and completely prehistoric," Barkley confidently said.

Around the bend, they came upon a herd of striped horses migrating north.

LION
Leopard
Elephant
Rhino
Cape Buffalo

"The Zebra is classic and chic ... black and white just like Henley," The Baroness chimed.

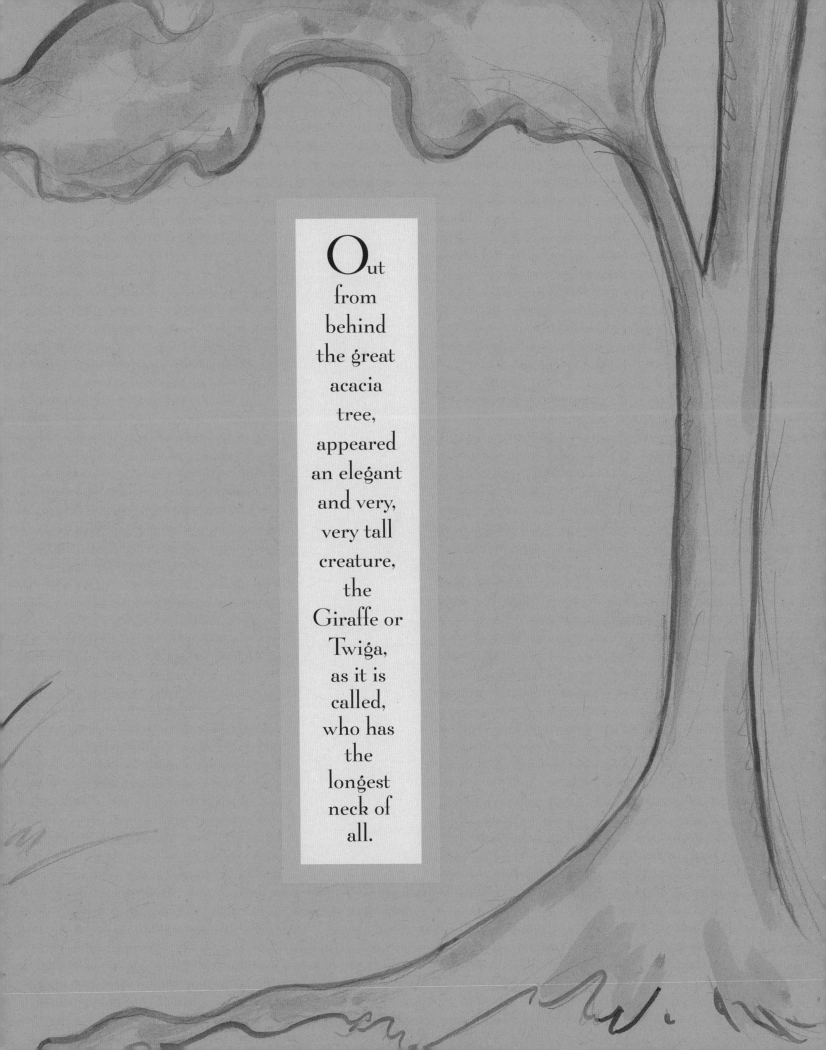

Out
from
behind
the great
acacia
tree,
appeared
an elegant
and very,
very tall
creature,
the
Giraffe or
Twiga,
as it is
called,
who has
the
longest
neck of
all.

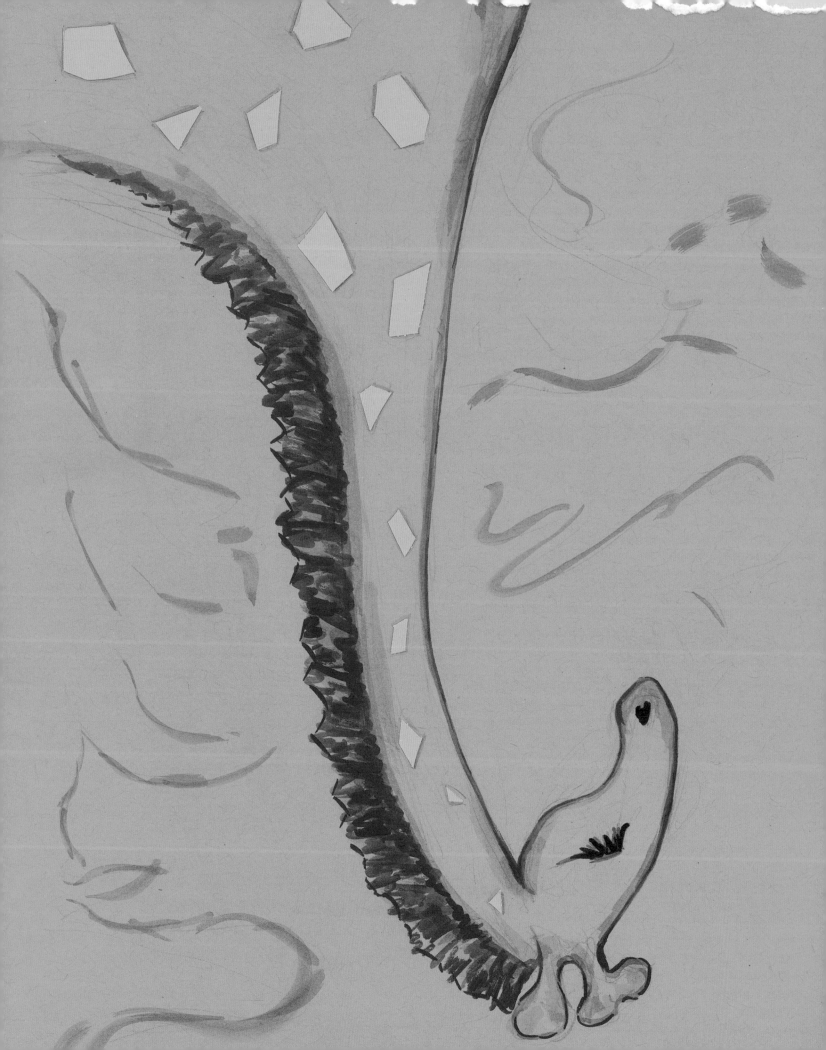

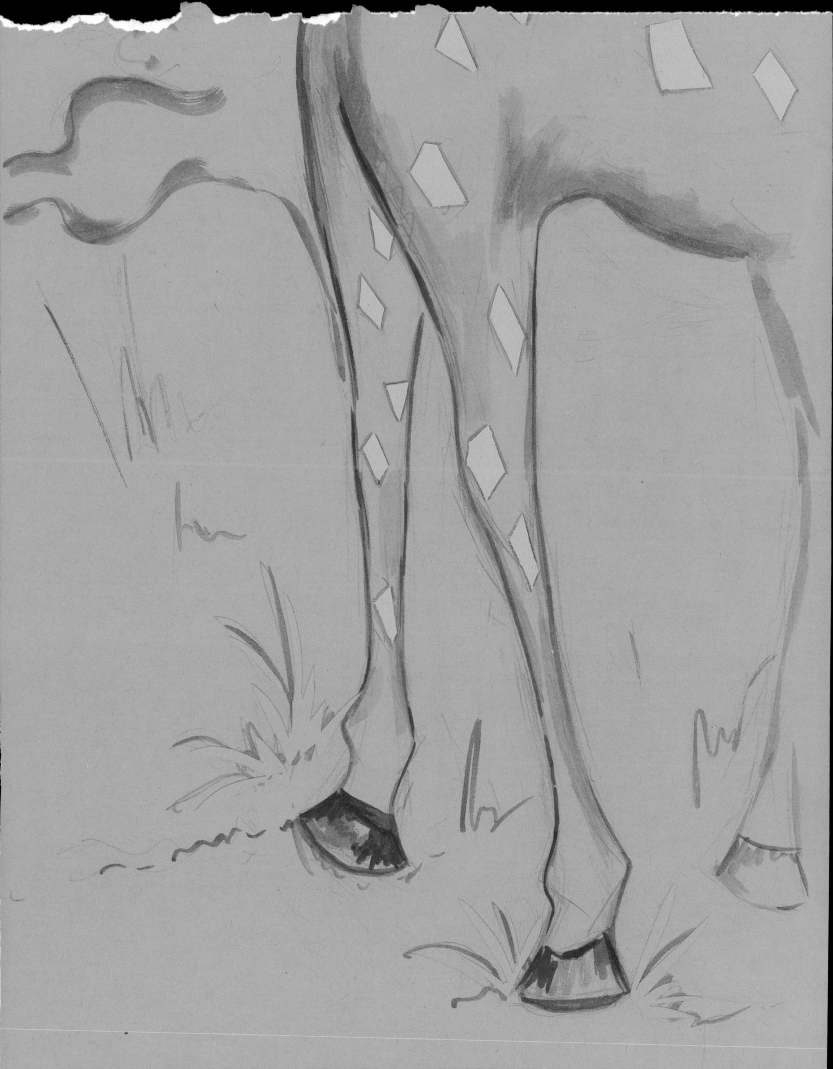

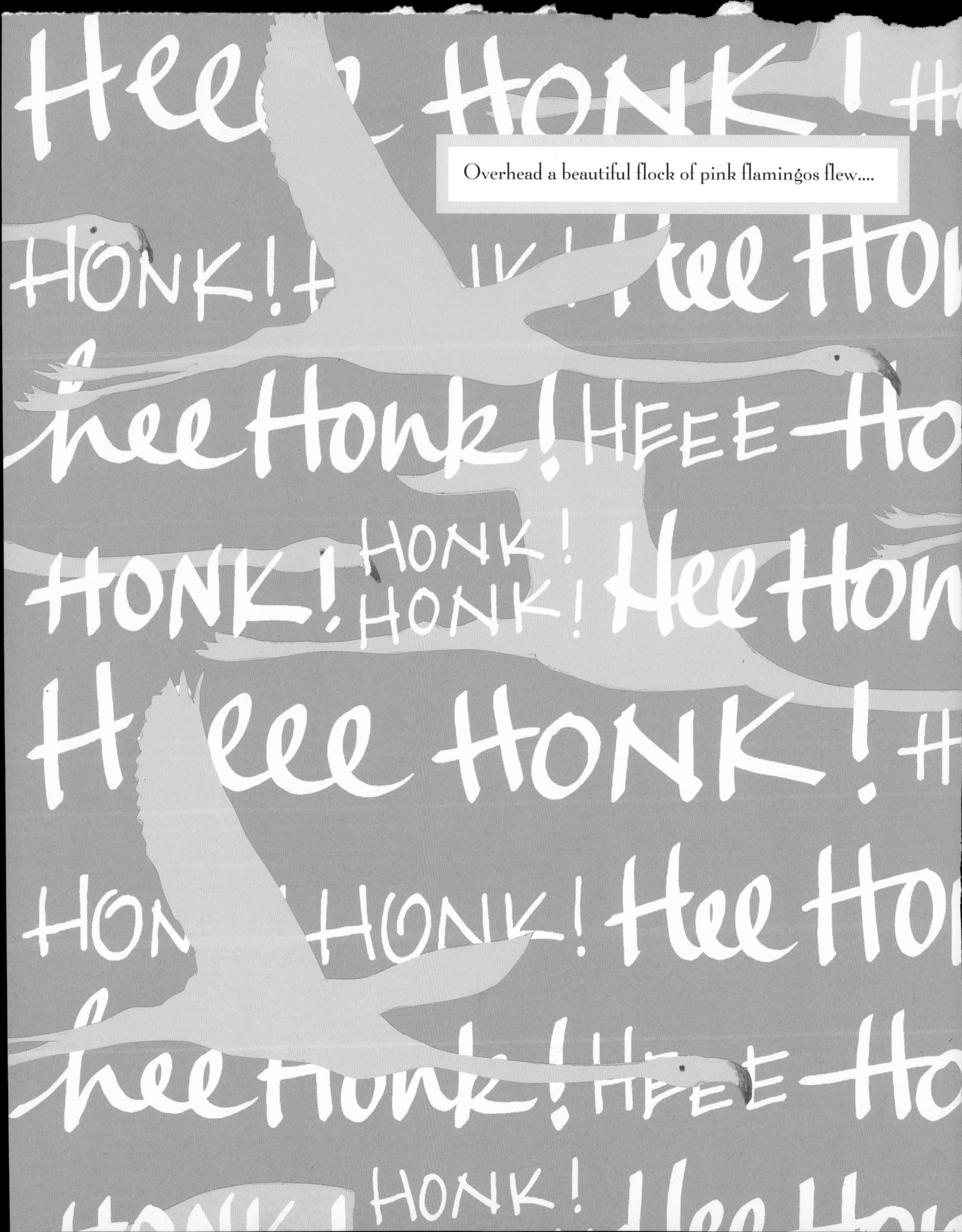

HEEE HONK! He

HONK!

hee Honk! HEEE Ho

HONK! HONK! Hee Hon
HONK!

Heee HONK! H

HON K! HONK! Hee Ho

hee Honk! HEEE Ho

HONK! Hee Ho

Overhead a beautiful flock of pink flamingos flew....

Honk! hee Honk!
Hee Honk! HONK
Hee Honk!
Hee Honk! Honk Honk
Honk! hee Honk!
Hee Honk! HONK
HONK! Hee Honk!

At last, they pulled up to a grassy knoll. Directly in front of them sat a large animal camouflaged in the luscious green fringe...

A LION!

Henley could not believe his eyes, for out of the grass climbed the biggest cat he had ever seen! Terrified, Henley began to tremble and shake.

"Really darling, don't be afraid, why he is the friendliest lion on the Serengeti Plains." The Baroness turned to Henley and said. "Come along, I will introduce you. Here kitty kitty..." The Baroness called out, "Purrsnickety..."

Then she gave Henley a little nudge towards the lion and asked, "Purrsnickety dear, could you be a fellow and teach him to bellow?"

Pleasantly Purrsnickety wiggled his whiskers and began to purr when suddenly...

He let out a deafening...

ROOOOOOAR!!!

Then to everyone's astonishment,
a wild thing happened...

Henley proudly sat up tall, why he was not afraid at all, because deep down inside he always knew, that he was a courageous little lion dog too!!!

And so with great vigor and valor and a quick shake of his coat, Henley proudly let out a lionhearted bark, followed by a

GLORIOUS,

WONDROUS,

THUNDEROUS,

RHINOCEROS SIZED...

Roar!

Beaming with pride...

They did it again!

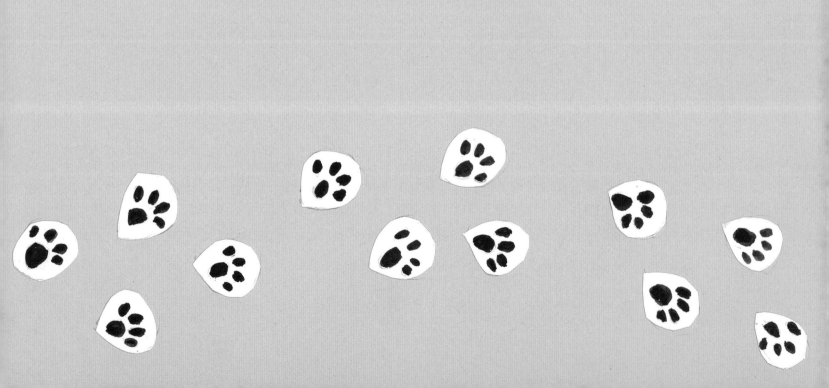